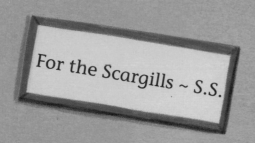

For the Scargills ~ S.S.

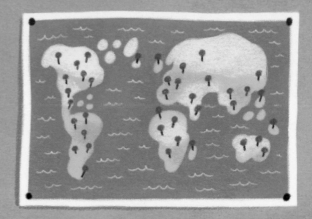

To my wonderful children,
Josie and Oscar ~ L.S.

tiger tales
5 River Road, Suite 128, Wilton, CT 06897
Published in the United States 2023
Originally published in Great Britain 2023
by Little Tiger Press Limited
Text copyright © 2023 Suzy Senior
Illustrations copyright © 2023 Lucy Semple
ISBN-13: 978-1-6643-0032-3
ISBN-10: 1-6643-0032-5
Printed in China
LTP/2800/5028/0423
10 9 8 7 6 5 4 3 2 1

www.tigertalesbooks.com

SANTARELLA

by
Suzy Senior Illustrated by
Lucy Semple

tiger tales

One snowy winter evening,

when the moon was bright and high,

the stars were sparkling gently;

there was magic in the sky.

But Cinderella sat alone.
Her work was never done,
while **EVERYBODY** else was
out there, busy having fun!

Her grumpy, bossy sisters left the house a **TOTAL** mess!

They'd ordered,
"Clean the messy floors!"

and "Mend my sparkly dress!"

And even "Clean my hamster cage!"
and "Paint that bathroom wall!"

And **THEN**, to make it even worse,

they'd waltzed off to . . . a **BALL!**

The sisters both had clever plans:
to meet the prince—and **YES**—
to somehow make him **MARRY** them
. . . and be a real **PRINCESS!**

But back to Cinderella,

in the kitchen, on her own,

about to watch a boring

Christmas movie on her phone.

"I wish," she whispered sadly,

"*I was going out as well.*"

And **THEN** she heard a **JINGLE**

and a **BUMP** as something fell!

The chimney seemed to wobble,
and there came a little yelp.
"OH, WOW!" gasped Cinderella,
and she rushed over to help.

"An actual **FAIRY GODMOTHER?**
Oh, really, could it be?"

"A fairy **WHAT?**" said Santa Claus.
"Oh, sorry, no—it's **ME!**

But **OUCH** . . . I have a problem,
and it seems to be my back.
I think I've pulled a muscle,
and I **CANNOT** lift this sack."

"Oh, dear!" cried Cinderella,
  "well, I do not have much planned.
I'm good with heights and animals—
  why don't I lend a hand?"

"Fantastic! Thanks!" beamed Santa Claus.
"Then let's be on our way.

You'll need a special hat to wear—
I have one in the sleigh."

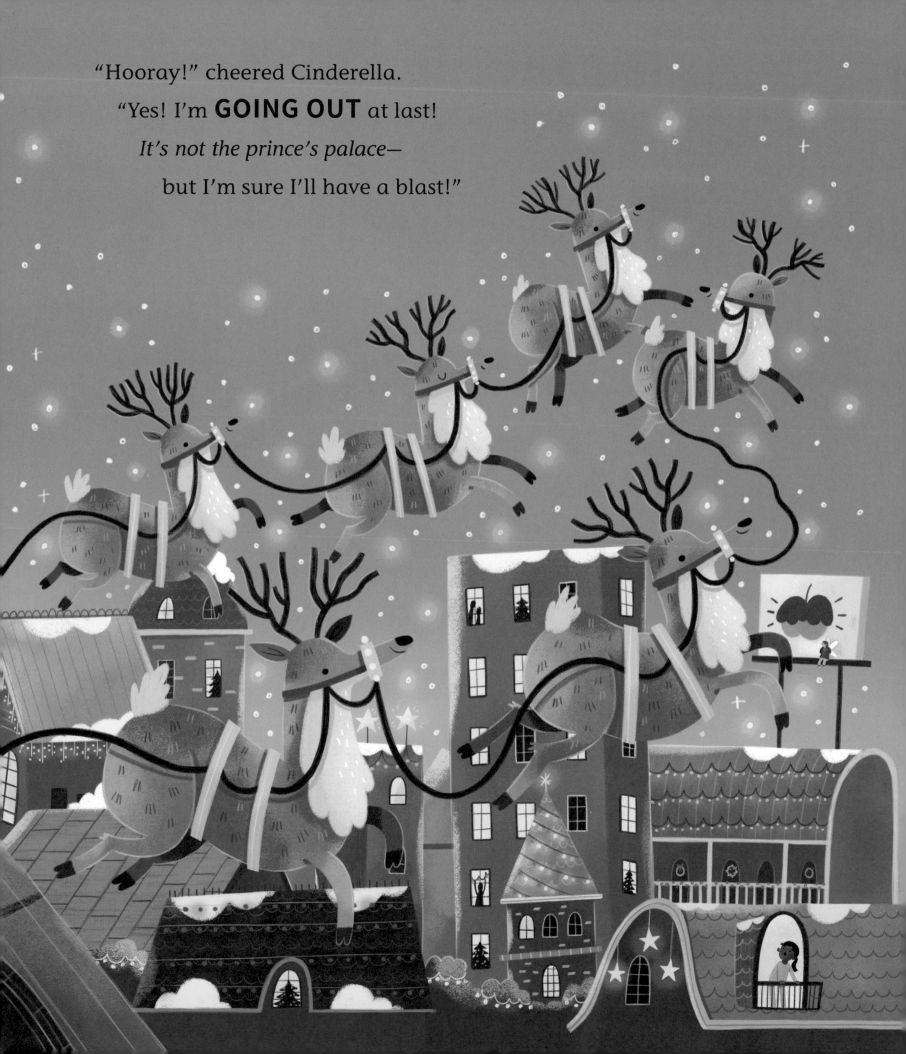

"Hooray!" cheered Cinderella.
"Yes! I'm **GOING OUT** at last!
It's not the prince's palace—
but I'm sure I'll have a blast!"

They gave out gifts around the world—

through Paris,

Bath,

and Cork.

They stopped by Iceland,

Canada,

Las Vegas,

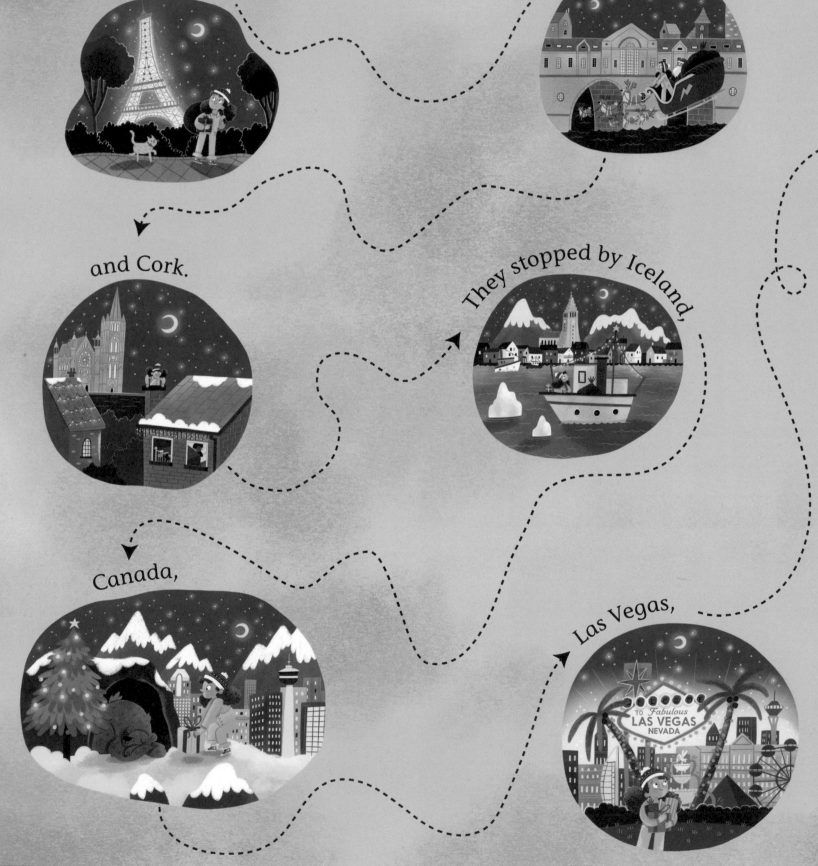

and New York.

Through Rio,

then the Nile,

and Nairobi,

and Kathmandu,

the job was done in record time—
and much more fun with two!

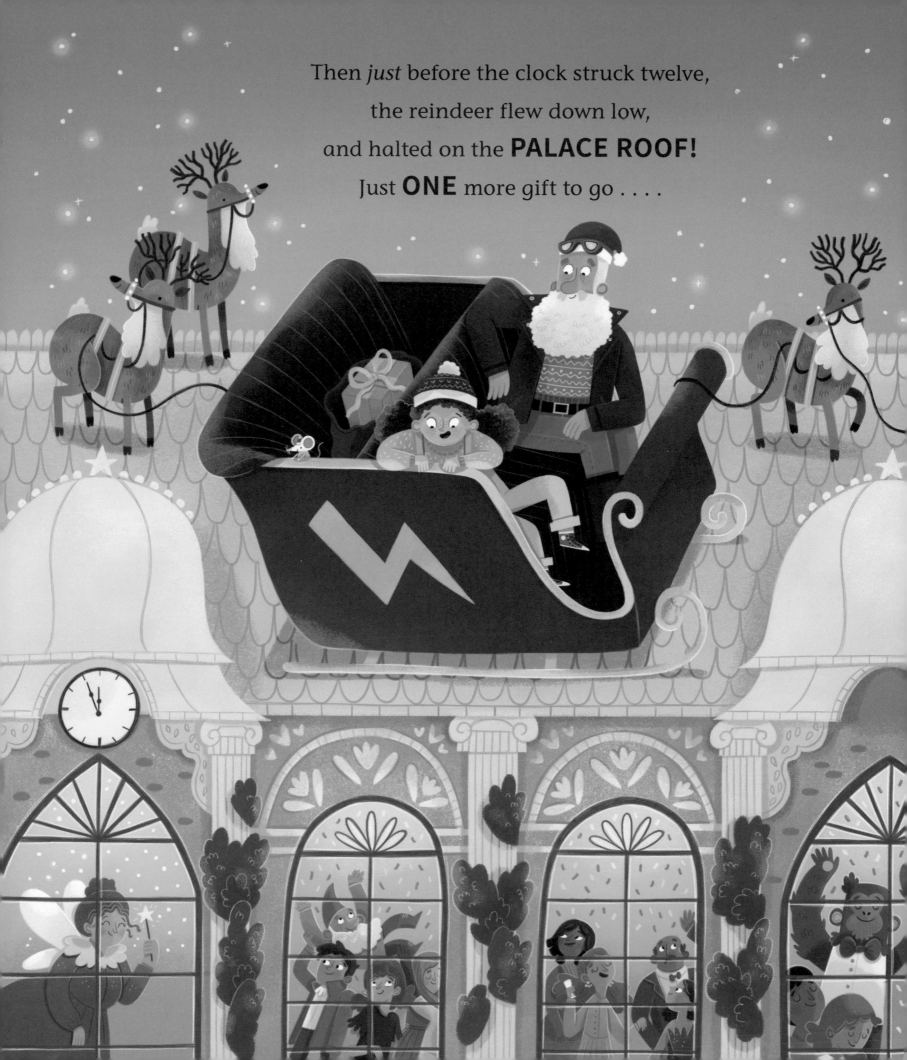

Then *just* before the clock struck twelve,
the reindeer flew down low,
and halted on the **PALACE ROOF!**
Just **ONE** more gift to go . . . .

"For **YOU!** Some fancy party shoes!"
said Santa with a grin.
"The party isn't over yet—
I'm sure they'll let you in!"

So Cinderella fixed her hair
and clutched the slippers tight.

She shimmied down the drainpipe
in the frosty moonlit night . . .

and peeked inside the ballroom, where the guests all danced and twirled.

"It's magical," she pondered, "but I'd rather see the **WORLD!**"

She climbed up next to Santa,
put the hat back on, and said,
"There's **SO** much I could **DO** out there!
I'd love a lift instead.

But first, I need to pack my things.
Can we stop by my house?

I need to get my bag of tools,
my lizard, rat, and mouse."

Then off she went adventuring,
through jungles,

lakes, and hills!

She's seen the sights,
made great new friends,
and learned some awesome skills.

She's even met a unicorn and
fixed his injured knee.

She's painted schools,
built mermaid pools,

and trimmed a giant's trees.

She's helped a dragon clean its teeth

and fixed a fairy's van.

If someone needs a problem solved—
then Cinderella **CAN!**

But every year she's always back
in time to load the sleigh.

Will Santarella visit **YOU?**

Perhaps she's on her way!